KU-140-001

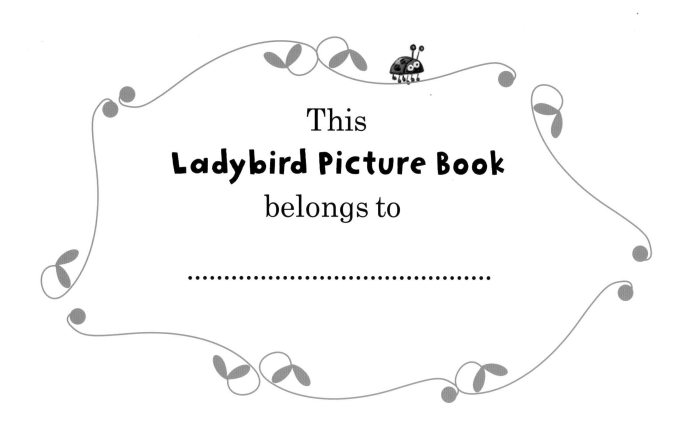

This
Ladybird Picture Book
belongs to

....

LADYBIRD BOOKS

UK | USA | Canada | Ireland | Australia
India | New Zealand | South Africa
Ladybird Books is part of the Penguin Random House group of companies
whose addresses can be found at global.penguinrandomhouse.com.

www.penguin.co.uk   www.puffin.co.uk   www.ladybird.co.uk

First published 2015
This Ladybird Picture Books edition published 2019
004

Copyright © Ladybird Books Ltd, 2015, 2019

Printed in China
A CIP catalogue record for this book is available from the British Library

ISBN: 978–0–241–38435–0

All correspondence to:
Ladybird Books, Penguin Random House Children's
One Embassy Gardens, 8 Viaduct Gardens, London SW11 7BW

Ladybird Picture Books

The Wizard of Oz

BASED ON THE CLASSIC TALE BY L. FRANK BAUM

retold by Rone Randall ★ illustrated by Ailie Busby

Dorothy lived in Kansas, America, with Uncle Henry and Auntie Em. Her little dog, Toto, also lived with them.

Dorothy and Toto were in the house together when along came some very nasty weather!

A big storm blew the house up high, way up into the sky!

When the house came down, Dorothy looked all around.

She said to Toto, "I'm not sure, but I don't think we're in Kansas any more."

Underneath the house,
two shoes were sticking out.

Standing and looking at Dorothy was a crowd of little people.

"We are the Munchkins," they said. "The Wicked Witch was mean. Now that she's dead, will you be our queen?"

Hooray! Hooray!

Dorothy shook her head and said, "I can't stay. I want to go home. Can you show me the way?"

"No," said the Munchkins. "But maybe our friend the Good Witch can."

"Go to the Emerald City and find the Wizard of Oz," said the Good Witch. "Wear these magic silver shoes.

The wizard will help you!

But you need to be quick, there's no time to lose.
Follow the road made of yellow bricks. You'll be
there in just two ticks!"

Dorothy and Toto set off down the yellow brick road. Soon they met a scarecrow.

"My head's full of straw," he complained. "What I really want is a brain!"

"We're going to see the Wizard of Oz," said Dorothy. "Maybe he can give you a brain."

Dorothy, Toto and the scarecrow set off.
Soon, they met a tin man.
Dorothy told him, "You look smart!"

"But I'm unhappy," he said, "because I have no heart!"

Come with us!

"We are going to see the Wizard of Oz," said Dorothy. "Maybe he can give you a heart."

Further along the road, they met a frightened lion.

"Everything I see and hear makes me shake and shiver with fear!" said the lion. "I need some courage!"

"Maybe the Wizard of Oz can give you some courage," said Dorothy.

The friends walked and talked until they came
to the Emerald City. What a wonderful sight!
It looked very pretty.

It was the strangest place they had ever seen.
Everything was sparkling and bright green!

Have you ever seen so much green?

A guard took Dorothy and her friends to see the wizard.

The wizard sat in a great big chair and asked them all why they were there.

"I want a brain," said the scarecrow.
"I want a heart," said the tin man.
"I want some courage," said the lion.
"And I just want to go home," said Dorothy.

The wizard put new stuffing inside the scarecrow's head. "You will feel better now you have a brain," he said.

Thank you!

And he put a red heart in the tin man's chest.
"It's a kind heart," he said. "This is the very best!"

Then he gave the lion a special magic drink. "This will give you courage, I think."

Dorothy stood there quietly, feeling all alone.
"Please," she said to the wizard, "will you help
me to get home?"
The wizard replied, "Just do as I say, and the
magic shoes will take you away!

Click your heels three times, and say where you want to go."
Dorothy did as he said.

With a whoosh and a whirl, through the air she swirled.

All at once Dorothy and Toto were back in Kansas!
Auntie Em hugged her tight and said, "Where
have you been?"
"To the Land of Oz," said Dorothy.
"Let me tell you what we've seen!"

I've been far away, but I'm home to stay!